D0021219

Graphic Novels Available from PAPERCUTZ

Graphic Novel #1
"Prilla's Talent"

Graphic Novel #2
"Tinker Bell and the
Wings of Rani"

Graphic Novel #3
"Tinker Bell and the
Day of the Dragon"

Coming Soon:

Graphic Novel #4
"Tinker Bell to the Rescue"

Graphic Novel #5
"Tinker Bell and the
Pirate Adventure"

Disney Fairies graphic novels are available in paperback for $7.99 each; in hardcover for $12.99 each.
Please add $4.00 for postage and handling for the first book, and add $1.00 for each additional book.

Please make check payable to NBM Publishing. Send to:
Papercutz, 40 Exchange Place, Suite 1308, New York, NY 10005
Or call 800.886.1223 (9-6 EST M-F)
MC-Visa-Amex accepted

www.papercutz.com

#3 "Tinker Bell and the Day of the Dragon"

Contents

PAPERCUTZ™

NEW YORK

"The Cobweb"
Script: Teresa Radice
Revised Dialogue: Stefan Petrucha
Layout: Elisabetta Melaranci
Pencils: Andrea Greppi
Inks: Marina Baggio
Color: Litomilano

"The Fox and the Fairies"
Script: Giulia Conti
Revised Dialogue: Stefan Petrucha
Layout: Emilio Urbano
Pencils: Manuela Razzi
Inks: Marina Baggio
Color: Litomilano
Page 18 Art:
Pencils: Manuela Razzi and Emilio Urbano
Inks: Roberta Zanotta
Color: Andrea Cagol

"Fairy Riddles"
Script: Augusto Machetto
Revised Dialogue: Stefan Petrucha
Layout and Pencils: Elisabetta Melaranci
Inks: Marina Baggio
Color: Stefania Santi
Page 31 Art:
Pencils: Bruno Enna
Inks: Elisabetta Melaranci
Color: Andrea Cagol

"Talents After a Fashion"
Script: Carlotta Quattrocolo
Revised Dialogue: Stefan Petrucha
Layout and Pencils: Elisabetta Melaranci
Inks: Marina Baggio
Color: Stefania Santi
Page 44 Art:
Pencils and Inks: Elisabetta Melaranci
Color: Andrea Cagol

"Day of the Dragon"
Script: Augusto Machetto
Revised Dialogue: Stefan Petrucha
Layout: Elisabetta Melaranci
Pencils: Cristina Giorilli
Inks: Marina Baggio
Color: Litomilano
Page 57 Art:
Pencils: Andrea Greppi
and Emilio Urbano
Inks: Marina Baggio
Colors: Andrea Cagol

Chris Nelson and Caitlin Hinrichs – Production
Michael Petranek – Editorial Assistant
Jim Salicrup – Editor-in-Chief

ISBN: 978-1-59707-128-4 paperback edition
ISBN: 978-1-59707-129-1 hardcover edition

Printed in Singapore. July 2010
by Tien Wah Press PTE LTD
4 Pandan Crescent
Singapore 128475

Distributed by Macmillan.

First Printing

IT'S THAT TIME OF YEAR WHEN PIXIE HOLLOW BUSTLES WITH ACTIVITY IN PREPARATION FOR QUEEN CLARION'S ARRIVAL DAY!

THE COBWEB

FOR ON THAT DAY, EACH FAIRY GIVES THE QUEEN A SPECIAL GIFT...

...BASED ON HER OWN *TALENT!*

SO, PRILLA, WHAT ARE *YOU* GOING TO GIVE THE QUEEN?

SINCE I'M LUCKY ENOUGH TO BE AN *HONORARY MEMBER* OF ALL THE TALENT GROUPS, I WANT TO TAKE ADVANTAGE OF THAT...

"...AND JOIN QUEEN CLARION'S *HELPER FAIRIES!*"

GLAD TO HAVE YOU, PRILLA!

WAIT UNTIL THE QUEEN SEES WHAT A *SPECIAL* JOB WE'LL DO ON THIS ROOM!

IT'LL BE GREAT!

BUT IT ALREADY *IS* GREAT! THE WALLS ARE ENCHANTING... THE FLOOR, AMAZING! NOT TO MENTION THE BED!

- 7 -

- 9 -

- 10 -

- 13 -

BACK IN PIXIE HOLLOW, A FRIEND'S HEART FILLS WITH CONCERN...

IT'S DARK AND THE QUEEN'S PARTY IS READY TO START!

BUT PRILLA, FIRA, AND BECK AREN'T BACK! I HEARD THEY WERE LOOKING FOR A GIFT, BUT THEY'RE SO LATE!

I SHOULD *TELL* SOMEBODY...

BACK IN THE FOREST, THINGS ARE DARK, BUT NO LONGER SO DANGEROUS.

AW! THE SPIDER'S AFRAID OF US! HE'S A PRISONER, TOO! I FEEL IT!

HUH? HOW'S A SPIDER GET CAUGHT IN ITS OWN WEB?

YEAH, BECK, HOW?

"OH, HE WAS PROBABLY SPINNING HIS *FIRST* WEB, AND NOT BEING AN EXPERT..."

ALL IT TOOK WAS A GUST OF WIND TO...WRAP THINGS UP ON THE POOR GUY!

WE CAN'T JUST LEAVE HIM OR *YOU* UP THERE!

PRILLA, YOU *SPECIALIZE IN RIPS,* DON'T YOU?

- 16 -

THE FOX AND THE FAIRIES

SPLASH

SNIFF
SNIFF

YOU MEAN OL' FOX! *MY WINGS ARE SOAKED!* HOW CAN I FLY NOW?

HE CAN'T UNDERSTAND YOU! HE'S A FOX AND YOU'RE NOT AN ANIMAL-TALENT FAIRY!

I KNOW! COME ON, LET'S HIDE IN THAT OLD LOG!

YELLING JUST MADE ME FEEL BETTER! NOT AS GOOD AS SEEING *YOU* THOUGH! THANKS FOR SAVING MY LIFE!

WE'RE NOT SAVED YET! THANK ME LATER!

- 23 -

- 29 -

FAIRY RIDDLES

ATTENTION ALL FAIRIES! OUR DEAR PRILLA'S HAD A WONDERFUL IDEA!

WE'RE GOING TO HAVE A SPECIAL *TREASURE HUNT!*

FANTASTIC! I'M UP FOR THAT! HOW ABOUT YOU, *DULCIE?*

SOUNDS SWEET AS A COOKIE!

IT'S SPECIAL BECAUSE IT'S ALSO A *RIDDLE* CONTEST! THE RIDDLE WILL TELL YOU WHAT TREASURE TO BRING BACK!

AH-HAH! SO WE'LL *ALSO* BE HUNTING FOR ANSWERS!

THE RIDDLES WE USE SHALL BE FROM THE BIG BOOK OF FAIRIES!

WOW! THAT'S WHERE WE FAIRIES HAVE *ALWAYS* KEPT *ALL OUR SECRETS!*

YES! FOREVER AND EVER! IT'S GOT ADVICE, CURIOSITIES, FACTS, LEGENDS, PROVERBS, COOKING TIPS...

AND RULES ABOUT *INTERRUPTING!* MAY I CONTINUE, *BECK?*

OOPS! I'D FLY BACKWARD, QUEEN CLARION...

TO BEGIN, I'LL READ THREE RIDDLES! RIDDLE ONE: "IT'S LIKE RAIN, BUT IT'S HARD. AND IF I CATCH IT... IT DISAPPEARS!"

"IT'S ROUND, BUT DOESN'T ROLL. VIOLET, BUT HAS NO PETALS!"

AND LAST BUT NOT LEAST: "IT FLIES, THEN IT DOZES, TASTES GREAT AND HAS THE COLOR OF THE SUN!"

IT'S SUPPOSED TO BE HARD! *SNOW* IS SOFT, REMEMBER?

THAT'S RIGHT! I SAW A PICTURE OF IT IN THE BIG BOOK ONCE...

ICE IS HARD, THOUGH, RIGHT? HOW ABOUT THE ICE-COLD CAVES! THEY SAY THERE'S ALWAYS *ICE* IN THERE!

AND THE ICE COMES FROM *RAIN!* NICE! GLAD I THOUGHT OF IT!

BUT RANI REMEMBERS THAT THE BIG BOOK IS FULL OF CREEPY LEGENDS ABOUT THE ICE-COLD CAVES...

THEY'RE COLD! AND DARK! AND... AND...NO ONE I KNOW HAS EVER GONE INSIDE...

BETTER YET! THAT MEANS I'LL BE THE FIRST!

NOT TO WORRY! IF ANYTHING IS IN THERE, IT *CAN'T* BE AS FAST AS I AM! BACK IN A *FLASH!*

BRRR! IT *IS* COLD...

- 37 -

- 42 -

SOON IT'S TIME FOR THE *TRY-ON* SESSIONS...

SO, WHERE IS IT? SHOW ME PLEASE! I CAN'T WAIT!

FIRA! RANI! YOU LOOK *FABULOUS!*

THANKS! THESE DRESSES TAKE INSPIRATION FROM OUR TALENTS...

...LIGHT FOR FIRA AND WATER FOR ME!

AND ME? WHAT ABOUT ME? CAN I SEE MY *DRESS?* PLEASE, PLEASE, PLEASE?

UMM... WELL...

GEE... WE...

...HAD SOME... *PROBLEMS...*

PROBLEMS? BUT YOU'RE SO... TALENTED!

YES, WELL, YOU SEE... THE DRESSES TAKE INSPIRATION FROM EACH FAIRY'S *TALENT*...

AND *YOU'RE* THE *ONLY* FAIRY WITH A MAINLAND-VISITING TALENT...

WHICH MEANS NONE OF *US* HAVE EVER *SEEN* THE MAINLAND! SO WE HAD TO *GUESS!*

HEY... YOU REALLY LOOK...

...GREAT...

IT MAY NOT BE *EXPRESSIVE*, BUT IT'S ELEGANT!.

THAT'S OKAY! IT'S NOT YOUR FAULT IF I HAVE...

...A TALENT NO ONE CAN *SEE!*

PRILLA! COME ON, *WINGS UP!*

!!!

TuEVENING, JUST BEFORE THE BIG PARTY...

❊SIGH!❊ WHAT BOTHERS ME MOST IS NOT BEING ABLE TO *EXPLAIN* MY TALENT!

YOU DON'T HAVE TO! WE ALL KNOW HOW *IMPORTANT* IT IS AND HOW *UNIQUE* YOU ARE!!

IT'S THANKS TO *YOUR* TALENT THAT THE CLUMSIES SEE *YOU* AND *BELIEVE* IN US!

OH, FIRA...

...THANK YOU SO, SO...!

...WHAT? WHAT IS *THAT*?

A BUBBLE-MESSAGE FROM RANI, FOR YOU! TOUCH IT!

PRILLA, FLY TO THE SEWING-TALENT WORKSHOP *RIGHT AWAY!* IT'S *URGENT!*

POP.

- 55 -

DAY OF THE DRAGON

IN PIXIE HOLLOW EVERYONE WORKS TOGETHER, WITH EVERY FAIRY PLAYING THEIR PART.

GARDEN-TALENT FAIRIES KEEP THE FLOWERS LUSH AND BEAUTIFUL.

GET THOSE PETALS WATERED, GIRLS! THE SUN'S WORKING OVERTIME, SO *WE* SHOULD TOO!

WHILE POLISHING-TALENT FAIRIES BRING A SPARKLE TO THE DAY.

SHINE THOSE DOORKNOBS! EVERY *DROP* OF SUNLIGHT SHOULD BE REFLECTED!

BEAUTIFUL DAY, *QUEEN CLARION!*

IT CERTAINLY IS! AND HOW *LUCKY* WE ARE TO *HELP!*

- 59 -

- 65 -

- 66 -

SO EVERYTHING *STILL* SMELLS LIKE BURNT ASH!

THERE'S THE BIMBIM TREE! THE ROOTS COVER THE CAVE HOLDING KYTO!

OH, MY POOR WEE NOSE! THIS SOOT'S WORSE THAN DUST!

I THINK... I'M GONNA... ≥ACHOO!≤

SHHH!

KYTO HAS *GREAT* HEARING! IF YOU HAVE TO SNEEZE DO IT IN A WHISPER!

THAT'S THE EASY PART! THE HARD PART IS FIGURING OUT *HOW* TO GET A PIECE OF THE ROOT!

THE BIMBIM TREE IS SO SUPER-HARD IT'S *IMPOSSIBLE* TO CUT!

A WHISPER-SNEEZE?

YOU CAN SEE WHERE KYTO TRIED TO *BURN* HIS WAY OUT WITH HIS FIERY BREATH!

- 68 -

I EVEN HEARD SOMEONE SAY, "OH, MY POOR WEE NOSE!" AND THEN SNEEZE!

THAT WOULD BE *ME!* DARN!

NOW, WHAT KIND OF HOST WOULD I BE IF I LET MY GUESTS CATCH *COLD?* SHALL I TURN UP THE *HEAT?*

WHOOSH

NO, WE'RE FINE, REALLY!

YIEE! THIS BEE IS SO OUT OF HERE!

WHA--?

SOOT! WE NEED SOOT, PRILLA!

IF YOU SAY SO, BUT I DON'T THINK IT'S A GOOD... *ACHOO!*

HURRY! *FLY WITH ME!*

Discover the stories of
Tinker Bell and her fairy friends!

Prilla and the Butterfly Lie

Queen Clarion's Secret

The Trouble with Tink

© Disney Enterprises, Inc.

COLLECT THEM ALL!
Available wherever
books are sold.
Also available on audio.

RANDOM HOUSE
CHILDREN'S BOOKS

LISTENING
LIBRARY

www.randomhouse.com/disneyfairies
www.disneyfairies.com

WATCH OUT FOR PAPERCUT𝗭™

Welcome, friends, to the third phantasmagorical DISNEY FAIRIES graphic novel from Papercutz. I'm Jim Salicrup, the Editor-in-Chief and one of those folks the fairies in Pixie Hollow call "clumsies." I'm here to talk to you about DISNEY FAIRIES and Papercutz—to tell you about everything that's new and exciting. Well, the news is so stupendous, so sensational, I can barely contain myself, so I better get right to it…

If you enjoyed the DISNEY FAIRIES DVDs, "Tinker Bell" and "Tinker Bell and the Lost Treasure," as much as I did, then you're going to be thrilled to find out that the third DISNEY FAIRIES DVD is in stores now! Yes, "Tinker Bell and the Great Fairy Rescue" is out now, and it's just as much fun as the first two were! Now, some of you may be wondering why I'm mentioning that here in the DISNEY FAIRIES graphic novel. I'll tell you why—because not only is "Tinker Bell and the Great Fairy Rescue" available as a DVD, it's also a graphic novel available from Papercutz!

As a comics editor, I'm also a comics fan and a comics collector. I'm even on the board of the Museum of Comic and Cartoon Art (www.moccany.org) in New York City because I love comics so much. And one of my favorite comics is the comicbook adaptation of PETER PAN originally published in 1952. That's where Tinker Bell made her comicbook debut! As wonderful as the original movie is—with such incredible animation, perfect voice acting, and unforgettable songs—there's a certain charm about having the same story in a comicbook that's indescribably special. That's why I'm so excited that Papercutz will be publishing "Tinker Bell and the Great Fairy Rescue" as a graphic novel.

And what a graphic novel it is! "Tinker Bell and the Great Fairy Rescue" is published at a bigger size than the DISNEY FAIRIES graphic novels—it's a big nine inches tall and a dainty six inches wide. And every comics page is devoted to telling "Tinker Bell and the Great Fairy Rescue"—it's a story so big and magical it fills up the entire graphic novel. We're so excited about this that on the following pages we're providing a very special preview of "Tinker Bell and the Great Fairy Rescue," but keep in mind that the actual graphic novel will be bigger, bolder, and brighter than the pages presented here. We just wanted to give you a little idea of what we're talking about.

There's just enough room to remind you that we want to know what you think of the DISNEY FAIRIES graphic novels. Email me at salicrup@papercutz.com or send a letter to us at: Disney Fairies, PAPERCUTZ, 40 Exchange Place, Suite 1308, New York, NY 10005. Also, be sure to visit www.disneyfairies.com for all the latest news direct from Pixie Hollow. And whatever you do, don't forget about the next DISNEY FAIRIES graphic novel! You'll get to see the encounter we're all eagerly waiting for—Vidia meets Captain Hook! It's in DISNEY FAIRIES #4 "Tinker Bell to the Rescue"!

Until then, this is Jim the honorary sparrow man wishing you Faith, Trust—and Pixie Dust!

Jim

WHEN SUMMER COMES, THE FAIRIES RIDE THE BREEZES TO THE *MAINLAND.* THAT'S WHERE THE *CLUMSIES* (WHICH IS WHAT THEY CALL PEOPLE LIKE YOU AND ME) LIVE!

SO MUCH TO DO AND SO MANY FAIRIES, EACH WITH A TALENT TO HELP REAWAKEN THE *SEASON.*

LIKE *WATER* FAIRY SILVERMIST, WHO MAKES SURE THE PONDS ARE CRYSTAL CLEAR...

GARDEN FAIRY ROSETTA, WHO HELPS THE FLOWERS STRETCH AND BLOOM...

LIGHT FAIRY IRIDESSA, WHO PUTS A SPARKLE ON THE SUNFLOWERS...

AND *ANIMAL* FAIRY, FAWN, WHO TEACHES BABY BIRDS TO FLY!

EVERY SUMMER, IT'S THE SAME, BUT FOR SOME, SUCH AS *TINKER BELL*, IT'S THE *FIRST* TIME.

HEY, *TINK!* READY FOR YOUR FIRST SUMMER ON THE MAINLAND?

ABSOLUTELY! IT'S SO BEAUTIFUL OUT HERE, *TERENCE!*

THERE IT IS, TINK! *FAIRY CAMP!*

HI, GUYS!

EVERY SUMMER, WHEN THEY ARRIVE, THE FAIRIES AND SPARROWMEN, LIKE *CLANK* AND *BOBBLE*, ALL SET UP A BASE.

IT'S EASIER TO WORK IN THE COOL AND QUIET BENEATH THE LEAVES, AWAY FROM *PRYING* EYES.

FAIRY CAMP ISN'T OUT IN THE OPEN... WE NEED TO STAY *HIDDEN* FROM HUMANS!

WE DO?

ER... NEED ANY HELP WITH THAT WAGON?

NOPE! SHE'S RUNNING FINE...

TINK, A TINKER-TALENT FAIRY, IS USUALLY *PLEASED* TO SEE HER INVENTIONS WORKING PROPERLY...

OKAY, GLAD TO HEAR IT!

BUT NOW IT LEAVES HER WITH *NOTHING* TO DO!

I *NEED* TO TINKER!

WHOA, YOU JUST GOT HERE! TAKE IT EASY!

HERE'S YOUR SUPPLY! I'VE GOT TO DELIVER PIXIE DUST TO OTHER FAIRY CAMPS...

AND DON'T WORRY! YOU'LL FIND SOMETHING TO FIX!

I *HOPE* SO...

Don't miss "Tinker Bell and the Great Fairy Rescue" Graphic Novel – available at booksellers everywhere!